Magic
Animal Friends

D1051868

For Darcie Littley

Special thanks to Valerie Wilding

No part of this publication may be reproduced, stored in a retrieval system, or transmitted in any form or by any means, electronic, mechanical, photocopying, recording, or otherwise, without written permission of the publisher. For information regarding permission, write to Working Partners Limited, Stanley House, St. Chad's Place, London WC1X 9HH, United Kingdom.

ISBN 978-0-545-68642-6

Series author: Daisy Meadows

All rights reserved. Published by Scholastic Inc., 557 Broadway, New York, NY 10012, by arrangement with Working Partners Limited. Series created by Working Partners Limited, London.

SCHOLASTIC and associated logos are trademarks and/or registered trademarks of Scholastic Inc. MAGIC ANIMAL FRIENDS is a trademark of Working Partners Limited.

12 11 10 9 8 7 6 5 4 3 2 1   15 16 17 18 19 20/0

Printed in the U.S.A.   40
First printing, June 2015

Lucy Longwhiskers
Gets Lost

Daisy Meadows

Scholastic Inc.

Shining House

Sunshine Meadow

Blossom Briar

Toadstool Café

Goldie's Grotto

Toadstool Glade

Mrs. Taptree's Library

Library

Friendship Tree

Maze

Silver Spring

Buttercup Grove

Lighthouse

Map of Friendship Forest

Ace Air Travel

Windmill

Mr. Cleverfeather's Inventing Shed

Muddlepups' Den

Treasure Tree

Sparkly Falls

Featherbills' Barge

Waterwheel

Entrance to the Caverns

Swamp

Grizelda's Tower

Can you keep a secret? I thought you could!

Then I'll tell you about an enchanted wood.

It lies through the door in the old oak tree,

Let's go there now—just follow me!

We'll find adventure that never ends,

And meet the Magic Animal Friends!

Love,
Goldie the Cat

Contents

CHAPTER ONE

A Golden Visitor

Lily Hart stepped into the long yard, breathing in the scent of the dewy grass. In the distance, nestled behind a grove of trees, was the barn her parents had turned into the Helping Paw Wildlife Hospital. Lily shrugged a vest over her green striped dress, then picked up the bucket of lettuce

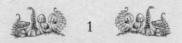

leaves waiting by the back door. Swinging

it over her arm, she walked over to a

large pen with a wire fence. At the end of

the pen was a wooden hutch.

"Breakfast time!" Lily called. A pink, whiskery nose poked out from one of the hutch's doors, then another. Soon three rabbits were hopping toward Lily. Two of them had bandages on their paws and the other had a bandage over its ear.

Lily opened the top of the pen and tipped the lettuce leaves into a bowl.

"Eat up," she murmured. Her bobbed dark hair had fallen across her face, and Lily tucked it behind an ear as she watched the rabbits nibble the leaves. *They're almost better now*, she thought. *Soon they'll be ready to go back to their burrow.*

A flash of movement from the row of houses across the road caught Lily's eye. One of the front doors had opened and out came a blond girl in denim shorts, leggings, and a pink hoodie.

Lily smiled. It was Jess Forester—her best friend!

Jess checked that the road was clear and hurried to the garden gate. She grinned as Lily ran to meet her.

"First day of vacation!" said Jess as the two friends hugged. "You know what would make this summer extra amazing? Helping in the hospital every day!"

Like Lily, Jess adored animals, and she loved living across from the Hart family.

Lily clapped her hands together. "Then let's get started! I just fed the rabbits, but the other animals need their breakfasts, too."

The girls passed the grove of trees where the Harts kept injured deer. A fawn was skipping around happily on three legs. His fourth leg was wrapped in a plaster cast.

"Dad fixed his leg yesterday," Lily explained. "I helped."

"Looks like you did a good job!" Jess patted the pocket of her shorts, where she kept her mini-sketchbook and pencil. "I'll have to draw him later."

They entered the barn, smelling the clean hay and fresh sawdust.

Mrs. Hart was standing by a hutch. "Just the helpers I need!" she said with a smile. Her jeans were tucked into a pair of muddy boots, and her dark hair was piled into a messy bun. "Could you feed these fox cubs for me?" she asked. "The poor things were found all alone."

Lily grabbed two pairs of thick gloves, and Jess fished in her pocket for a hairband to tie back her blond curls. They were ready for work!

Soon the fox cubs were drinking greedily from feeding bottles, just like babies! When they finished, Lily entered the feed time in the hospital's computer.

"Can you fill the water bottles in the hutches, please?" asked Mrs. Hart. "All except the end one—that hutch is empty. I'm off to check on the baby badgers.

They're very happy in the burrow we built. They seem to think it's a real one!" She bustled out of the barn.

Lily and Jess filled the bottles from little watering cans, speaking softly to the squirrels, mice, and hedgehogs as they worked.

Finally, Jess said, "That's all of them."

But suddenly, Lily saw something move in the end hutch. *Funny*, she thought. *Mom said it was empty.*

"Look, Jess," she whispered, opening the door and peering inside.

In the shadows at the back of the hutch

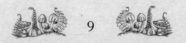

nestled a cat. Its pointed ears twitched at the sight of the girls.

"That's weird," said Jess. "How did a cat get in?"

"Magic?" suggested Lily. They both laughed.

With a mew, the cat leaped out of the hutch. It had golden fur and eyes as green as spring leaves.

"She's so pretty," said Jess, tickling the soft fur on the cat's head. "Lily, doesn't she look just like that cat who came in last year with the hurt paw?"

Lily looked thoughtfully at the cat. "She does! I wonder if it's her. Let's check."

Lily went to the computer to check the patient records. She clicked through a few pages, then gasped.

"Look!" she said, pointing to an old entry on the screen. It read:

> **Patient: Female cat.**
>
> **Appearance: Gold fur, green eyes.**
>
> **No collar—maybe a stray?**
>
> **Notes: Arrived with an injured paw.**
>
> **Healed well. Took a real liking to Lily and Jess! Patient then disappeared.**

Beneath the entry was a photograph of the golden cat.

"We were right!" said Jess. "I wonder why she came back today?"

The cat jumped down from the hutch and curled around the girls' legs, purring.

"She doesn't look sick," said Lily, "so that can't be the reason. It's a mystery!"

The cat moved toward the barn door, stopped and looked back at the girls, then darted outside!

"Come on!" called Jess. "Let's catch that cat—before she disappears again!"

CHAPTER TWO

The Magical Tree

Lily and Jess ran outside. The golden cat sprinted across the Harts' lawn toward Brightley Stream, which ran along the bottom of the yard.

"That's weird," Jess panted as the girls followed. "Cats usually keep away from water."

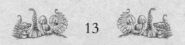

Lily's dad had put stepping-stones in the stream so people could cross safely. The cat sprang onto the first stepping-stone. Then she looked over her shoulder at the girls and mewed.

Lily's dark eyes were wide. "She isn't running away," Lily said. "I think she wants us to follow her!"

With a flick of her golden tail, the cat leaped onto the next stone. The girls

quickly jumped after her. On the other
side of the stream, in Brightley Meadow,
stood a huge oak tree. Even though it
was the middle of summer, the tree had
no leaves. Jess's dad was a science teacher,
and he'd told them it was dead.

But as the cat ran to the tree, something
amazing happened. Leaves sprang from
every twig, bright green and shimmering
in the sunshine, as if they had been

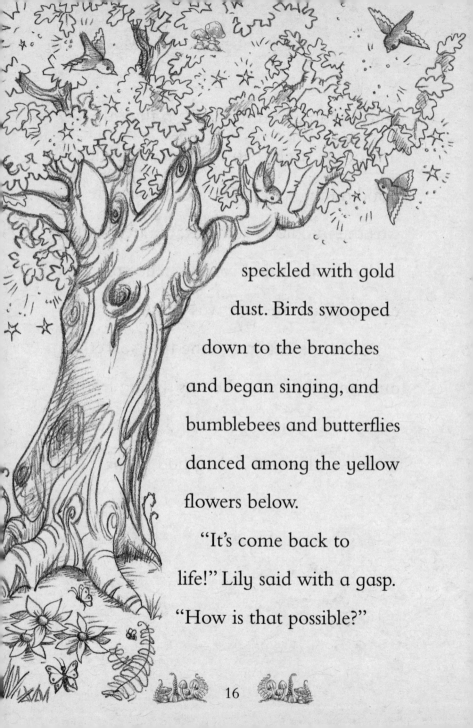

speckled with gold
dust. Birds swooped
down to the branches
and began singing, and
bumblebees and butterflies
danced among the yellow
flowers below.

"It's come back to
life!" Lily said with a gasp.
"How is that possible?"

Jess rubbed her eyes. She couldn't believe what they were seeing!

The golden cat was rubbing around the tree trunk, pawing at some strange marks.

Jess kneeled to stroke her silky fur. "I know this sounds crazy, but I think the cat has something to do with this!"

Lily nodded, her eyes wide. "Look! There's writing carved into the trunk."

Jess crawled around the tree, reading the letters. "Friend . . . ship . . . For . . . est . . ."

The cat meowed and pawed at the letters once more.

"Maybe she wants us to say it louder?"

Jess guessed. "FRIENDSHIP FOREST!" she shouted.

But the cat just meowed again. She first rubbed Lily's leg, then Jess's, and pawed at the letters.

"I know!" cried Lily. "She wants us to read it together!"

Both girls said, "Friendship Forest!"

Instantly, a small door appeared in the trunk! It was as high as the girls' shoulders and in the center was a handle shaped like a leaf.

"Wow!" said Jess. Her eyes shone as she gripped the handle.

Lily reached toward it, too, then hesitated. "Do you think we should open it?" she asked warily. "We don't know what's on the other side."

"Exactly!" said Jess with a grin. "Let's find out!"

Lily twisted the handle, and the little door swung open. A shimmering golden light poured out of the tree.

The cat looked up at the girls. Her green eyes seemed to beg them to follow, then she bounded inside the tree.

Jess held out her hand to Lily. "Ready?" she asked with a smile.

Lily grinned and took Jess's hand. "Let's go!"

Taking a deep breath, they bent down. As they squeezed through the door, their skin tingled all over.

The girls blinked as the golden glow faded. They were standing in a clearing in the middle of a sunlit forest.

The leaves on the tall trees shimmered, and flowers nodded their colorful heads in the gentle breeze. The ground was covered in soft, springy moss.

"This is impossible," Jess said. "How can all this fit inside a tree trunk?"

Lily took Jess's hand again. She was trembling with excitement. "There is an explanation for all this . . ."

Jess nodded. Together, both girls cried, "Magic!"

"This is amazing!" Jess said, grinning. "But why did the cat bring us here?" She glanced around. "Where'd she go?"

Lily peered behind some pink flowers with petals like tissue paper, hoping to catch a glimpse of golden fur. A familiar scent drifted up from the blooms.

"These smell like cotton candy!" she exclaimed. "Even the flowers are magical!" Then something odd caught her eye.

Inside a hollowed-out tree trunk stood a little cottage.

"Look!" Lily cried.

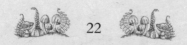

"Sweet!" said Jess. "But what's a playhouse doing here?"

A curtain at one of the windows twitched. Jess shook her head. Surely there couldn't be anyone inside the cottage . . . Could there?

As the girls gazed around, their eyes widened. More little cottages were dotted around the clearing. Some were nestled among tree roots, and one was half underground, with a mossy roof. Tables and chairs as high as the girls' knees stood outside a wooden cabin with white spots on the roof. A sign said TOADSTOOL CAFÉ.

A door at the side of the café suddenly slammed shut. From inside came the sound of worried voices.

Lily gasped. "Someone's living in these little buildings," she said. "But who?"

CHAPTER THREE

Friendship Forest

"They're the animals of Friendship

Forest," said a voice.

The girls turned around, trying to work

out where the voice had come from. To

their astonishment, they saw that the

golden cat had reappeared. Standing

upright on her hind legs, she reached

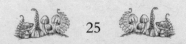

almost to the girls'
shoulders—and she
was smiling at them!
Jess noticed that she
had a glittery scarf
looped around her
neck, too.

After a few moments, Jess found her
voice. "You can talk," she said, shaking her
head in amazement. "And you've grown!"

The cat laughed, her green eyes
sparkling. "Actually, you two have shrunk!
You became smaller when you stepped
through the door in the tree," she said.

"Oh, so that's what the tingling feeling was!" said Jess.

The cat nodded. "My name's Goldie. Welcome to Friendship Forest, Jess and Lily!"

Lily gasped. "You know our names!"

Goldie nodded. "I couldn't talk to you in your world," she explained, "but I understood what you were saying. All the animals here walk upright and talk, just like me."

The girls gazed around in delight. "A forest full of talking animals," said Lily. "This is amazing!"

Goldie put her paws to her mouth and called, "Come out, everyone! Meet Jess and Lily!"

A little door between two tree roots opened and a mole peeked out. From another door came a squirrel wearing a bowtie. His tail swished as he hopped over to the girls. Door after door opened and more animals appeared, gathering around Lily and Jess.

"I'm Harry Prickleback," said a little hedgehog as he waddled out from a clump of cotton candy flowers.

"It's lovely to meet you," said Lily, bending down to tickle Harry's nose and making him giggle. She could hardly believe she was talking to a hedgehog!

A kitten wearing a backpack scampered over. "I'm Bella Tabbypaw," she said.

"What kind of animal are you? You're too tall to be a rabbit and you haven't got any wings, so I don't think you're birds . . ."

"We're girls!" Jess stroked Bella under her soft chin. She could feel the rumble of her purr.

"None of the animals have seen people before," Goldie explained. "That's why they were hiding."

A bird almost as tall as the girls flapped down from a tree. "Captain Ace, at your service," he said. He wore a flying helmet with a badge reading ACE AIR TRAVEL and raised one wing in a salute.

"He's a stork!" Lily whispered to Jess.

Jess saluted Ace back.

Two rabbits came out of the Toadstool Café, one in a waiter's jacket and one brushing flour from her apron. "Well, I say, how lovely to meet you!" said the waiter. "We're Mr. and Mrs. Longwhiskers."

Running out behind them came a young rabbit with a purple ribbon around her neck. She was so small that

Lily thought she'd fit in the palm of
one hand.

"I'm Lucy
Longwhiskers," the
rabbit said in a rush.
"You're really tall.
How old are you?
Do you live in Friendship Forest like
me? How—"

Goldie interrupted her with a laugh.
"This is Lily and Jess's first visit to
Friendship Forest. Would you like to help
me show them around?"

Lucy gave a happy squeak. "Can I?
Can I?" she asked her mom and dad.

"Of course," said Mrs. Longwhiskers.
"Stay close to Goldie, and don't get into
any trouble!"

The animals bustled around as the girls waved good-bye.

"Bye!" squawked Captain Ace. "Come back soon!"

The girls glanced excitedly at each other as they set off through the trees with Goldie and Lucy. Sweet scents drifted up from the flowers and beads of dew twinkled on the mossy ground like tiny stars.

"You've been at Helping Paw before, haven't you, Goldie?" asked Lily as they walked. "We both recognized you. Why did you bring us here?"

"Ever since I was a tiny kitten, I've been able to go between Friendship Forest and your world," Goldie explained. "I was in your world when I hurt my paw, and a kind lady took me to your wildlife hospital."

Goldie told Lucy how Lily and Jess had looked after her while she recovered.

Lucy's eyes were wide and shining. "That was so kind! I'm happy that you're in Friendship Forest." She bounded on ahead.

"I never forgot you," Goldie said. "I've

always thought that if I needed help,
I could call on you two."

"Are you in trouble, Goldie?" Jess asked.
"What's wrong?"

"I think Friendship Forest is in
danger." Goldie lowered her voice so
Lucy wouldn't hear. "A few days ago, I
was on my way home with a basket full
of berries when I saw a tall woman in a
cloak walking through the trees. I
was about to say hello, but then she
stopped to pick a flower. Its pretty yellow
petals went gray, then it turned to dust in
her hand!"

Lily gasped. "How horrible! But who was she?"

"I don't know." Goldie's whiskers trembled. "I'm worried she might harm Friendship Forest."

A shiver ran through Jess. They couldn't let that happen!

"Don't worry, Goldie," Jess said. "If this stranger tries anything, we'll stop her."

"You can count on us!" Lily said.

"Thank you," said Goldie, reaching up to hold the girls' hands in each of her forepaws. "Here we are! Welcome to my home!"

CHAPTER FOUR

Grizelda

The trees opened out to reveal a large,
mossy clearing in front of a cave. Set
into the front of the cave was a red
door with a little window in the shape
of the letter G.

Goldie beamed. "This is my grotto!"

Lucy hopped across the clearing, her

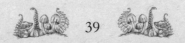

tiny white tail bobbing. "Look at the

Blossom Briar!" she said, sitting on her

back legs and peering up.

Lily and Jess followed Lucy's gaze.

Growing beside the cave was a bush

as tall as the forest trees. It was

covered in huge, colorful flowers as

fluffy as pom-poms.

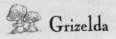

Lily gave a delighted cry. "It's beautiful!"

"The Blossom Briar is connected to every flower in Friendship Forest," Goldie explained. "As long as the Blossom Briar blooms, all the flowers in the forest will, too."

Jess ran to stand beneath the Blossom Briar's branches, giggling as a football-size yellow flower tickled her face. "It's like being inside a rainbow!" she called. She took out her sketchbook and started to draw the shape of the flowers.

Lily held Lucy up so she could sniff

a purple flower. The little rabbit was
quivering with excitement.

Then Lily spotted something strange.
An orb of yellow-green light was floating
above the Blossom Briar.

"What's that?" Lily asked.

Goldie's eyes went wide with alarm.
"I don't know, but I've got a bad feeling
about it. My fur's standing on end!"

They all watched the light float down.
It hovered in the center of the clearing,
casting an eerie glow. Lily could feel Lucy
trembling in her arms.

"Quick, hide!" said Goldie. She pushed

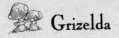

open the red front door and they

ran inside.

Through the window, the girls could see

the orb of light growing bigger, then ...

Cra-ack! It exploded into a shower of

green sparks.

The sparks faded

to reveal a tall,

thin figure wearing a

shiny purple tunic

over tight black

pants. Her high-

heeled boots had

sharply pointed toes,

and her long green hair swirled around her head. A black cloak hung from her shoulders.

"It's the woman I saw!" Goldie whispered.

Jess felt her tummy tighten into a knot. She glanced at Lily. She could tell from her friend's wide eyes that she'd had exactly the same thought . . .

"Goldie," Jess said, "I think that woman is a witch!"

Goldie frowned. "A witch? What are witches?"

"Bad people who do magic," Lily said.

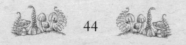

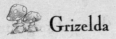

She felt an icy shiver ripple down her spine. "They're usually just in stories, but this one's real . . ."

Lucy squealed and ran to hide behind Goldie's bed.

Goldie swallowed. "Stay here."

She opened the door and stood in front of the witch. "You must leave Friendship Forest at once!" she cried.

The witch's thin lips curled into a smile, but her eyes glittered coldly. "I don't think so," she said with a sneer. "I've built a wonderful tower across the Wide Lake, full of darkness and cobwebs. When I climbed to the top, I saw this forest—and now I want it for myself!" She rubbed her hands together. "Of course, I'll have to get rid of all the animals first."

"No!" said Goldie bravely. "Friendship Forest is our home!"

Jess could see that the tip of Goldie's tail was trembling with fear. "We said we'd help Goldie," she told Lily. "Come on!"

Jess pushed open the door and the girls went and stood next to their friend.

"Goldie's right," Jess said, her fists clenched. "Witches don't belong here! Get out!"

The witch peered
down her thin nose
at the girls. "Well, what
have we here?" she said.
"Two silly little human
girls. You must be pretty stupid to think
you can get the better of Grizelda!"

The witch laughed. The sound echoed
around the clearing like terrible crashes
of thunder. Lily felt a cold wind whip
around her.

"Friendship Forest will be mine, and I
know how to get it," the witch snapped.
"I heard what you said about the

Blossom Briar, cat. Green is for hair, not leaves! I'll destroy it—then all the flowers in the forest will die. It will turn gray and miserable, and all the animals will leave!"

Lily shuddered. She couldn't imagine Friendship Forest without its beautiful flowers. "We won't let you, Grizelda!" she said, trying to keep her voice steady.

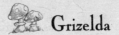

The witch gave another dreadful cackle. "You're too late. My helpers are already here to start work!"

At that moment, four hideous, lumpy creatures the same size as Lily and Jess crashed through the trees. They wore filthy, ragged clothes, and their fur was a patchwork of dingy green, washed-out

blue, and sickly yellow. They smelled like rotting cauliflower.

Grizelda clapped her hands as the creatures gathered around her. "Welcome, Boggits—my messiest and most loyal helpers. If you tear down the silly Blossom Briar, you can have that cave as your new home!" She turned to Goldie. "You'd better find somewhere else to live, cat. You and your humans can't stop me!"

And with that, Grizelda snapped her fingers and vanished in another shower of sparks.

CHAPTER FIVE

Bunny-napped!

The girls stared at each other in dismay.
Then Goldie bravely walked up to the
Boggits.

"I live in this grotto," she said politely.
"But I'm sure we can find you a new
home somewhere else."

The first Boggit shook his grubby head.

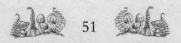

"Boggits been living in a mud pool by Grizelda's tower. This grotto be much better once Boggits make it good and messy!"

"But you can't steal Goldie's home!" Jess protested.

"Or hurt the Blossom Briar!" added Lily.

The second Boggit snorted. "Boggits not listen to nosy humans. I be starting with nasty flowers now."

"Ladies first, Pongo," growled a girl Boggit, elbowing him out of the way.

"Ow, Whiffy, that hurt!" yelled Pongo.

Whiffy took no notice. She jumped up at the Blossom Briar, ripping off a flower.

"Stop!" shouted Lily.

The Boggits just laughed. "Haargh! Haargh!"

"Now rip down them other flowers," shouted Pongo. "Come on, Sniff! Over here, Reek!"

"No!" shouted a little voice.

Lucy had come out of Goldie's grotto. The tiny rabbit's whiskers were quivering with fear, but she hopped up to the Boggits.

"Leave the Blossom Briar alone!" cried the little rabbit.

"Lucy, go back inside!" called Goldie.

But before Lucy could move, Pongo

scooped the rabbit up in his big, smelly

paw. Lucy squirmed, her ears shaking

with fright.

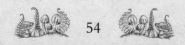

"Help!" she squeaked.

Jess clenched her fists. "Put her down!"

Goldie sprang at Pongo, reaching out for Lucy. But the Boggit dodged aside.

"Go, Pongo!" Whiffy yelled. "We show rabbit what happens when you mess with Boggits."

Clutching Lucy, Pongo ran off.

"After him!" yelled Jess.

The girls and Goldie followed as Pongo crashed through the forest. But the Boggit had gotten a head start, and soon he was far ahead of them.

"This way!" called Lily, leading her

55

friends around a bush with white flowers
that were shaped like stars. But when
they reached the other side, Pongo had
vanished among the trees.

Jess felt as if her heart had sunk into
her sneakers. "He could have taken Lucy
anywhere. How will we know where
to look?"

"There must be a clue somewhere,"
said Lily.

She peered around a tree while
Goldie sniffed the air for his horrible,
rotting smell.

"Nothing," the cat said.

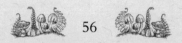

Jess wriggled right
under the bush,
but there was no
sign of Pongo or the
little rabbit.

"Do you think he
might have taken
Lucy into our world?"
Jess asked, rubbing mud from her leggings.

Goldie shook her head. "I can visit
the human world because I was born
there, but the other animals can't—and
you're the only humans who can visit
Friendship Forest." For a moment, her

57

worried frown faded and she smiled up at the girls. "Your love of animals makes you special, you see."

"So Lucy's somewhere in the forest," Jess said. "But where?"

Lily sat on a patch of moss, trying to think. Beside her, the star-shaped blooms nodded in the soft breeze. Most of them were as white as milk, but one was gray,

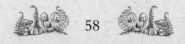

just like the flower Grizelda had turned

to dust. Then another of the white blooms

turned as dull as stone.

"Look!" Lily cried. "The flowers are

dying because the Boggits are hurting the

Blossom Briar."

With a gasp, Jess pointed to a patch

of yellow flowers. Lots of them were

gray, too.

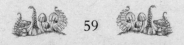

"This is terrible," said Goldie. "The sooner we find Lucy, the sooner we can stop the Boggits! If we don't hurry, all the flowers in Friendship Forest could die."

Almost all of the star flowers were gray now. But Lily noticed that one of them still had a purple, silky center . . .

Her heart racing, Lily picked out a scrap of material from the flower. "Look!" she cried. "This comes from Lucy's bow, doesn't it? The ribbon must be unraveling. Everybody look for scraps of purple fabric. The trail will lead us to Lucy!"

CHAPTER SIX

Mr. Cleverfeather

The girls and Goldie darted through
the forest. Lily spotted a second piece
of material.

"This way!" she called.

Soon, Jess found a third strand, then
Goldie saw another, beneath a tall tree.

"This must be the right way," she panted.

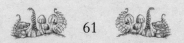

But that was the last scrap they found.

Jess groaned. "I can't believe it! We were so close."

They were all wondering what to do when a loud buzzing sound from above made them jump.

Jess looked up. "Watch out!" she cried, as hundreds of dead leaves showered down from the tree.

"Do you think it's Grizelda?" Lily asked, looking up anxiously. The thought of the witch lurking nearby made her shiver.

Buzzzz!

More leaves tumbled down. Jess darted

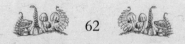

away and leaned against a tree. Beneath
her fingers, she felt the trunk move . . .

Jess spun around. The surface of the
trunk was rippling and twisting!

"Hey, look at this!" she called.

Lily and Goldie hurried over. A
staircase appeared on the tree, winding
around the trunk up into the branches.

"More magic!" Lily breathed.

"Maybe Lucy's up there," Jess
suggested. "Let's find out!"

She put one foot on the bottom step
and began to climb, with Goldie and
Lily close behind.

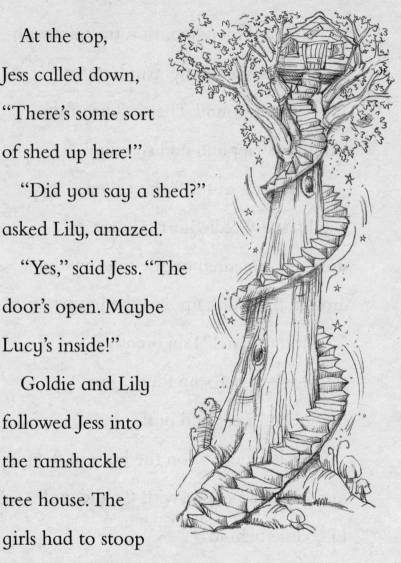

At the top,
Jess called down,
"There's some sort
of shed up here!"

"Did you say a shed?"
asked Lily, amazed.

"Yes," said Jess. "The
door's open. Maybe
Lucy's inside!"

Goldie and Lily
followed Jess into
the ramshackle
tree house. The
girls had to stoop

slightly because their heads touched the ceiling. It was gloomy, with leaves everywhere, and no sign of Lucy . . .

But there was an owl. He wore a striped vest with lots of little pockets, and a monocle fixed in front of one eye, like half a pair of eyeglasses.

"Yeeeek!" the owl screeched. He pressed a button on the long tube he held.

Buzzzz! It blew the leaves into a spin, making the girls and Goldie squeal.

"Yeeeek!" the owl screeched again. He dropped the tube and his monocle flew off.

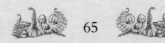

"Don't be scared!"
cried Goldie. "It's
me, Goldie, and my
friends, Lily and Jess!"
The owl felt around
the floor with his wing
tips. "Where's my monocle?" he wailed.
"I can't see properly without it."

Lily found it and gave it to him.

"Thank you," he said. "I do jolly pies."

"Jolly pies?" Jess wondered aloud.

"I think he means 'apologize'!"
said Lily.

"Girls, this is Mr. Cleverfeather," Goldie

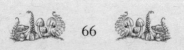

66

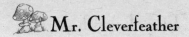

explained. "I think we've found his secret inventing shed!"

The girls gazed around. Half-finished gadgets, drawings, and tools covered every surface. A diagram labeled FOR TWINKLETAIL FAMILY showed plans for a double-decker stroller that held five baby mice on each level. Another was a machine for catching baby birds that fell out of their nests.

"What's the long tube for?" asked Lily, pointing to the contraption that Mr. Cleverfeather was holding.

"It's my latest invention," Mr. Cleverfeather said. "A beef lower.

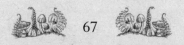

Er, I mean a leaf blower. Leaves get everywhere, you see, and mess up my inventions." He squinted at Jess and Lily. "What sort of creatures are you?"

"Jess and Lily are young humans," Goldie explained. "They're clever and brave."

"Most interesting," said Mr. Cleverfeather. "But why are you here?"

Goldie told him about Lucy, the Boggits, and the Blossom Briar.

"Have you seen Lucy?" Lily asked.

"I'm afraid not," said Mr. Cleverfeather.

Lily wasn't surprised. He didn't seem to have very good eyesight.

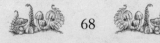

"You could try my telescope," Mr. Cleverfeather suggested. "Maybe you can spot the runny babbit—er, bunny rabbit." He opened the back door and led them onto a balcony.

Mr. Cleverfeather lifted a cover made of leaves stitched together, revealing a wooden telescope. Lily crouched down to look through it, scanning the forest in all directions. Suddenly, she caught sight of something moving at the top of a chestnut tree.

"It's Lucy!" she yelled. "But she's in a cage. Her ears are droopy and she looks so sad."

Jess and Goldie gasped as they took turns looking through the telescope at the little rabbit.

Faintly, Lucy's voice floated toward them. "Help! Please, someone help me!"

"She's really scared!" Goldie cried.

Jess clenched her fists. "Let's get her out of there, right now!"

"But she's so high up in that tree," Lily said despairingly. "We'll never reach her!"

CHAPTER SEVEN

Boggit Blaster

"Ahem. There is a way," said a voice.

"Mr. Cleverfeather!" said Jess, turning to see the owl standing behind them.

"You can use my pea-shoot laugh," Mr. Cleverfeather explained. "I mean, my secret path. Ta-da!" He swished back a curtain of willow fronds, revealing

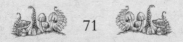

a wooden path covered in vines
that snaked through the treetops.

"A walkway!" cried Lily.

"It helps me get around," said
Mr. Cleverfeather. "My old wings
aren't what they used to be."

Thanking Mr. Cleverfeather, Goldie,
Jess, and Lily ran off along the walkway,
grabbing the wooden railings to keep their
balance. Soon they were close enough to
see Lucy huddled in a cage made from
sticks and rope.

"Help!" Lucy whimpered.

"We're here, Lucy!" Goldie called. "We'll get you out!"

When she saw them, Lucy's ears perked up. "Goldie and the girls! Hooray!" she shouted, hopping around on her tiny paws.

When they reached the cage, Jess tugged at the ropes that held the bars together—but they wouldn't budge. Lily and Goldie tried, too, but the ropes remained firmly tied.

Lucy's ears drooped back down. In a trembling voice, she asked, "Will I have to stay here forever?"

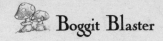

"Of course not!" said Lily. "We're going to save you." But she gave Jess and Goldie a worried look. How could they free the little bunny?

Goldie was examining the knots that held the ropes in place. "Pongo tied these really tightly. We need something to loosen them . . ."

Jess felt a fizz of excitement as an idea came to her. She took her pencil out of her shorts pocket and worked the tip into the bunched-up knot.

Goldie's green eyes gleamed as the knot fell apart. "Great job, Jess!"

Jess took one end of the rope, Lily the other, and together they undid the cage. The sticks came apart and Lucy bounded out onto the walkway.

"You rescued me!" she cried, her white tail bobbing as she hopped around their feet. "Thank you, Goldie! Thank you, girls!"

Lily kneeled down
to pick Lucy up.
She curled up in
the crook of Lily's
arm, her whiskers
twitching happily.
They hurried
back to Mr.

Cleverfeather's tree, where the owl gave

a delighted squawk. "Young Lucy! I'm

so happy to see you wit and fell—er, fit

and well."

Goldie's tail drooped. "We've rescued

Lucy," she said, "but how can we stop the

Boggits before they completely destroy
the Blossom Briar?"

Jess gave a cry of excitement. "I have
an idea! Mr. Cleverfeather, can we borrow
your leaf blower?"

Hiding behind a bush next to Goldie's
grotto, Jess got the leaf blower ready.
A horrible smell filled the air, like
filthy pond water mixed with stinky
sneakers and moldy cheese. Through
the bush's leaves, they could see the
Boggits stomping around the Blossom
Briar. Many of its flowers had been

ripped down and lay trampled around
the clearing.

Lucy trembled in Lily's lap and folded
her ears over her eyes.

"Don't worry," Lily whispered. "We'll
keep you safe."

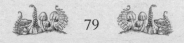

Sniff's dirty, multicolored fur bounced
as she clambered onto Whiffy's back so
she could reach more flowers. She tore
down a red one, yelling, "This be good
Boggit fun!"

Reek jumped up and gripped a branch
of the Blossom Briar that was covered in
yellow flowers. With a creak, it snapped
under his weight. "Haargh! Haargh!"
Reek laughed. He threw the branch into
the clearing, where Pongo jumped up and
down on it, crushing the petals.

Goldie's eyes flashed. "I think we've seen
enough," she whispered. "Hurry, Jess!"

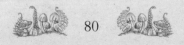

Jess pressed the leaf blower's button.

Buzzzz!

SWOOOSH!

A gust of air blew, sending trampled petals into a rainbow-colored whirlwind spinning around the Boggits.

"Uggy! Uggy!" Pongo cried.

"Nasty flowers in my fur!" shrieked Sniff. "Get them off!"

Reek yelled in panic. "Beastly petals in my pants!"

"Pooh! I smell like flowers!" Whiffy roared, brushing off blossoms. "Disgusting! Boggits must get out of here!"

Lily, Jess, and Goldie giggled. Even Lucy
peeped out when Jess gave another quick
blast, making the Boggits shriek.

"What's happening?" Lucy asked.

"The Boggits like dirt and nasty smells,"
Lily whispered, "so if we smother them
with pretty flowers, they'll go away."

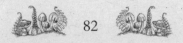

Buzzzz!

The shrieks and yells grew louder.

"Boggits, back to Grizelda's tower!"
Pongo bellowed. "Bath in mud pool will
take nasty flower smells away."

The horrible creatures thundered off
into the trees.

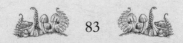

83

"Hooray!" yelled Jess and Lily. Goldie reached up and grabbed their hands, spinning them around in delight, while Lucy hopped beside them, her tiny white tail bouncing.

Then Jess noticed that a familiar orb of yellow-green light was zipping through the trees toward them ...

Goldie's fur stood on end. "Grizelda!"

CHAPTER EIGHT

Watch Out, Grizelda!

The orb of light burst into a storm of angry yellow sparks that faded to reveal Grizelda. Her green hair flicked and twisted like snakes.

Lucy dived back beneath the bush, but Jess, Lily, and Goldie stood their ground.

"Don't think that you've defeated me!"

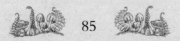

the witch screeched. "You've stopped the Boggits this time, but I'll find a way to take Friendship Forest for myself!"

Jess's legs were trembling, but she stepped forward. "It won't work, Grizelda," she said. "Whatever you try, we'll stop you!"

Grizelda stooped down low and narrowed her eyes. When she spoke, Jess could feel her cold breath. "Two girls and a cat are no match for me," she hissed. "You better watch out!"

She snapped her fingers and disappeared in another flash of sparks.

After a moment's silence, Lily spoke.
"Actually, it's Grizelda who better
watch out."

Jess nodded. "We'll help keep Friendship
Forest safe, Goldie."

The cat slipped a paw into each of
their hands. "I knew I was right about

you two," she said, smiling. "Come on, let's take Lucy home."

"And the Boggits ran away, covered in petals," said Jess, finishing the story of their adventure to all the animals at the Toadstool Café.

Mr. and Mrs. Longwhiskers pulled Lucy into a hug. "Thank you so much for rescuing her," Mr. Longwhiskers cried.

"Hooray for Goldie and the girls!" chanted Harry Prickleback and Bella Tabbypaw. "They stopped the witch!"

The other animals joined in while

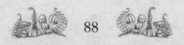

Captain Ace the stork flew a loop-the-loop above them.

Mrs. Longwhiskers disappeared into the café to make a celebration dinner, while Mr. Longwhiskers asked about the poor Blossom Briar.

"In time, its blossoms will grow back," Goldie said. "I'm afraid some of the flowers in the forest have been damaged, but most of them are safe."

After a little while, Mrs. Longwhiskers called, "Dinner's ready!"

The café tables were laden with delicious food. Mr. Longwhiskers poured

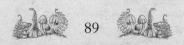

blackberry juice and strawberry soda into acorn cups. They ate honey sandwiches and rolls filled with watercress, cherry tomatoes, and sweet radishes. Next were slices of iced seed cake with cherries on top. Mrs. Longwhiskers said that the cakes were only cookie-size for Lily and Jess, so they could have a whole one each!

Just as they were feeling full, Captain Ace spluttered into his cup of strawberry soda. He'd spotted Mr. Cleverfeather coming out through the trees. "Well, I never!" the captain said. "We hardly ever see Mr. Cleverfeather these days!"

"A big cheer for Mr. Cleverfeather and his leaf blower," shouted Jess. "Hip, hip . . ."

"HOORAY!"

Jess gave the leaf blower back to Mr. Cleverfeather, and the old owl pressed the button by mistake, showering Lucy with cake crumbs.

"I say," said Mr. Cleverfeather.
"I do, er—"

"Jolly pies!" said Goldie, and everyone laughed while Lucy nibbled at the crumbs. Lily gave the owl a plate of sandwiches and seed cake.

"What a day!" Jess said, munching on her cake.

"It was amazing," agreed Lily. "But I think my mom will be wondering where we are. It's time for us to go home."

They said good-bye and Goldie led them to a beautiful tree with golden leaves close to Toadstool Glade.

"This is the Friendship Tree," Goldie said. When she touched a paw to the trunk a door appeared, just like the one in Brightley Meadow.

Lily looked serious. "Goldie, I think Grizelda meant what she said. She won't stop trying to make the animals leave the forest."

Goldie sighed. "You're right," she said. "She'll find another way to harm the forest. Maybe she'll

attack the Silver Spring, where the river starts, or the Treasure Tree, where we get our food . . ."

"Then we'll stop her," said Jess fiercely. "We promise!"

Goldie hugged each of the girls. "Thank you," she said. "As soon as Grizelda makes trouble again, I'll come and find you."

Lily opened the door in the tree.

"Good-bye, Goldie!" the girls chorused. "See you soon!"

They stepped into shimmering golden light. As it cleared, they found themselves back in Brightley Meadow.

"Did that really happen?" asked Lily.

"I think so," said Jess.

They glanced back. The door had disappeared, but they could still make out the letters carved into the tree trunk.

"It wasn't a dream," Lily murmured. "Friendship Forest is real."

"It must be so late," said Jess, checking her watch. She frowned. "Hey! It's the same time as when we left!"

Lily stared. "So time stood still while we were in Friendship Forest? Cool! Listen, Jess," she said. "Should we keep this our secret?"

"Of course!" said Jess. "Our very own magic animal friends. Who would believe us, anyway?"

They laughed and skipped over the stepping-stones, back to the wildlife hospital. As they walked through the gate, Lily's mom waved at them.

"Having a good morning?" she asked.

"Yes, thanks," said Lily. "The best start to the summer ever. So far it's been—" She looked at Jess.

They giggled and said together, "Magical!"

The End

Grizelda is still trying to take over Friendship Forest and now her horrible Boggits have played a mean trick on little Molly Twinkletail!

Join Lily, Jess, and Molly in the next adventure,

Molly Twinkletail Runs Away

Turn the page for a sneak peek . . .

Jess and Lily both drew in a sharp breath. The Boggits were talking about Molly Twinkletail!

Pongo thumped his chest. "Pongo was clever, telling her to fetch drinks from Sparkly Falls for Boggits."

Sniff laughed so much she nearly fell out of the tree. "Off mouse run to help. But mouse will never be able to do it. Haargh haargh!"

The Boggits whooped and jumped onto the ground. They ran around the Treasure Tree trunk, kicking squashed fruit at each other.

Jess, Lily, and Goldie stared at one another in alarm.

"Poor Molly," said Lily. "She just wants to help people—even the horrible Boggits. Now she's even farther from home. And all alone!"

Read

Molly Twinkletail Runs Away

to find out what happens next!

Puzzle Fun!

Can you spot the five differences between the
two pictures of Lucy Longwhiskers?

ANSWERS

1. Spot on toadstool missing
2. Whisker missing
3. Extra star and sparkle
4. Grass missing to Lucy's right
5. Tail of her bow is missing

Lily and Jess's Animal Care Tips

Lily and Jess love helping lots of different animals—both in Friendship Forest and in the real world.

Here are their top tips for looking after . . .

RABBITS

like Lucy Longwhiskers.

- If you have a pet rabbit, make sure they don't get bored! Hide treats around their cage and give them lots of toys to gnaw on.

- Don't forget to give your rabbit fresh water daily and the right food to keep them healthy.

- Make your rabbit's hutch cozy and fun by making lots of hideaway holes for them to snuggle up in—just like they would in the wild.

- If you are concerned about a sick-looking wild bunny, call your local wildlife animal hospital.

RAINBOW magic ™

Which Magical Fairies Have You Met?

- ☐ The Rainbow Fairies
- ☐ The Weather Fairies
- ☐ The Jewel Fairies
- ☐ The Pet Fairies
- ☐ The Dance Fairies
- ☐ The Music Fairies
- ☐ The Sports Fairies
- ☐ The Party Fairies
- ☐ The Ocean Fairies
- ☐ The Night Fairies
- ☐ The Magical Animal Fairies
- ☐ The Princess Fairies
- ☐ The Superstar Fairies
- ☐ The Fashion Fairies
- ☐ The Sugar & Spice Fairies
- ☐ The Earth Fairies
- ☐ The Magical Crafts Fairies

Find all of your favorite fairy friends at
scholastic.com/rainbowmagic

HiT entertainment

RMFAIRY11

RAINBOW magic™

SPECIAL EDITION

Which Magical Fairies Have You Met?

3 stories in each one!

- ☐ Joy the Summer Vacation Fairy
- ☐ Holly the Christmas Fairy
- ☐ Kylie the Carnival Fairy
- ☐ Stella the Star Fairy
- ☐ Shannon the Ocean Fairy
- ☐ Trixie the Halloween Fairy
- ☐ Gabriella the Snow Kingdom Fairy
- ☐ Juliet the Valentine Fairy
- ☐ Mia the Bridesmaid Fairy
- ☐ Flora the Dress-Up Fairy
- ☐ Paige the Christmas Play Fairy
- ☐ Emma the Easter Fairy
- ☐ Cara the Camp Fairy
- ☐ Destiny the Rock Star Fairy
- ☐ Belle the Birthday Fairy
- ☐ Olympia the Games Fairy
- ☐ Selena the Sleepover Fairy
- ☐ Cheryl the Christmas Tree Fairy
- ☐ Florence the Friendship Fairy
- ☐ Lindsay the Luck Fairy
- ☐ Brianna the Tooth Fairy
- ☐ Autumn the Falling Leaves Fairy
- ☐ Keira the Movie Star Fairy
- ☐ Addison the April Fool's Day Fairy
- ☐ Bailey the Babysitter Fairy
- ☐ Natalie the Christmas Stocking Fairy
- ☐ Lila and Myla the Twins Fairies

▬ SCHOLASTIC

Find all of your favorite fairy friends at
scholastic.com/rainbowmagic

HIT entertainment

RMSPECIAL14

Visit Friendship Forest, where animals can talk and magic exists!

Meet best friends Jess and Lily and their adorable animal pals in this enchanting new series from the creator of Rainbow Magic!

■ SCHOLASTIC

scholastic.com

MAGICAF1